swedish erotica – five novels
Original title: Feministisk erotik

Leopard förlag
Björngårdsgatan 15, Stockholm
www.leopardforlag.se
Print: BoD - Books on Demand
isbn 978-91-7343-969-5

swedish erotica

five novels

Lavender oil
M. Lanvin

The reward
Sayo Coimbra

The sex club
Malin Edholm

Summer night
Saga Becker

Pink desire
Ottilia E.

lavender oil

M. LANVIN

The air smells of laundry detergent and sunlight, outside the window clothes are hanging out to dry. The damp bathroom has begun to fill with steam. Condensation soon covers the mirror. I place the cigarette, half-finished, in the ashtray next to the toilet seat.

When I first moved to Italy I found this so liberating, everyone smoking everywhere, what a cliché. It didn't take long before I had a small ashtray in each room of the apartment.

The sound of the usual courtyard banter drifts in through the window and, from further away, the humming of cars and vespas. I close the brown shutters, leaving a crack to allow the heat of the sun to enter, but enough to block the view of curious neighbours. If I had been alone I wouldn't have bothered, there's something thrilling about the feeling of being observed while walking around naked.

It had been a lonely year, by choice. The days were spent in school, followed by evening sessions in front on the computer. At some point after midnight my back would begin to protest and I would close the laptop and go to bed. The few times I ventured out I had a beer down by the square, observing the groups of teenagers and their loud and confident flirting.

A loud tone pierces the apartment, the buzzer screams. I twist the knob on the bathtub faucet to turn the water off and walk out into the hallway. The feeling of the cold tiles beneath my feet makes my skin rise and I shiver. But soon the hot bath will warm me up, and so will you.

I press the button to open the gate and leave the front door ajar. On my way back to the bathroom I walk past the kitchen and finish the last of my coffee. Just as I reach the bathroom I see you enter. I pause for a second and observe you. You look up just as you close the door, locking it behind you. A huge smile spreads across your face when you realize that I'm naked. With your finger you signal for me to wait a second. You reach for something in your back pocket, a small bottle.

You bend down and place the bottle on the floor, sliding

it towards my feet. I put extend foot to catch it. It looks like lavender oil, the same kind we saw at the market last Sunday.

I turn around and bend down slowly to pick up the bottle.

I spread my legs slightly for you to be able to have a better look; my thick thighs, my round butt cheeks and my pussy are all exposed. I don't bother to look for your reaction; I already know how you will react. I know you must be hard already.

I walk into the bathroom and place the small bottle on the edge of the bathtub. I'm just about to step into the water as you approach from behind and pull me closer. You grab my hair, gathered in a bun, and hold me still while you kiss and lick my neck. Your cold hands caress my back and hold my hips in a firm grip. In truth, I hardly know who you are.

I know your body, but I don't even know what your voice sounds like. Even if I had been able to talk to you, I'm not sure I would have. There's something liberating about just communicating with our bodies.

You take my hand and direct me out of the bathtub, gesturing for me to sit down on the edge. I hesitate slightly when I feel the cold against my butt cheeks; the hot water is so tempting. You get down on your knees in front of me.

The green mosaic tiles must be hard against your legs. I place my hand against your face; your cheeks are clean shaven with a hint of stubble. You smell slightly of men's perfume and sweat.

You separate my legs carefully, your face is just a few inches from my pussy. You place both of your hands on the insides of my thighs and let them glide up towards my groin slowly. My pussy vibrates with excitement. You let your hands pause there, gently resting on the softest part of my inner thighs. I love when you make me wait like this, when you make me impatient.

You must notice that I'm cold, my nipples are hard and my legs are covered in goose bumps. The heat from the steam rises against my back. I want to slide down into the bathtub but your steady gaze keeps me still.

You bring your mouth closer to my pussy. I watch you, longing for your lips to reach my clitoris, but you stop. You take a deep breath and exhale hot, soft air all over my pussy, sending a shiver through my entire body. All I want is to press my thighs against your head, so that I finally get to feel you. But I resist. Instead I arch my back to get closer to you, but you pull back slightly. You're teasing me too much.

I stand up suddenly, I'm too cold. You're still on your knees, your head turned up to face me.

I don't hesitate, I straddle your face, burrying you between my thighs. Finally, your tongue is against my clitoris.

I grab your neck to help you support your head. Your tongue creates warmth and wetness as you hold onto my

4

ass. Your heat begins to spread through my body, I can feel the movement of the orgasm approaching. But if we were to stay in this position until I came your neck would get stiff, so I back away. You remain in the same position, your lips shining with the juice from my pussy. Even through your jeans I can see that you're hard. You probably also have that little wet and salty stain on your underwear, right by the tip of your penis.

I step into the bathtub, my cold feet sting as they enter the hot water. I let myself down into the water and place my head against the edge. My pussy is pounding. I need to keep my hands above the water or else I'm not sure I'll be able to resist the temptation of rubbing my fingers hard against my clitoris until I come.

You stand up and pull your shirt off. From your jeans pocket you pull out a cigarette and light it with my old lighter lying next to the ashtray. You sit down on the toilet seat and watch me as you draw the smoke from the cigarette deep into your lungs.

Your body's quite slender, but your shoulders are unexpectedly muscular. They look strong, as if you're used to labour. Your body's typically masculine, and you move like a clumsy man. Yet the way you sit is feminine, placing one leg over the other and locking your foot behind the calf.

You place your elbow on one knee and it looks so simple, so casual. I could never be so gracious, not with my figure. Perhaps you're a dancer?

You place the cigarette between your teeth and break into a smile. You unbutton your jeans and make room for your dick, placing one hand around it inside of your underwear.

My hand slips down below the water, how could I resist? I throw one leg over the edge of the bathtub, so that they're spread apart beneath the surface. You must be able to see quite well through the water because your gaze is fixed on my pussy. I glide my fingers down over the lower part of my stomach, down towards my clitoris. I see your hand begin to move slightly inside your underwear.

With my other hand I point towards your crotch, trying to signal for you to remove your briefs. You understand immediately, you pull your pants further down so that you can pull your dick out. A small drop gleams on its head. Your rough hand has a firm grip of your dick, which is thick and not too long.

I begin to rub my fingers against my pussy, my inner thighs vibrate as they always do when I'm really turned on. You watch me with a hungry gaze, your pretty brown eyes go back and forth between my face and my pussy.

All of the sudden a thought appears in my head, it's as if I can see myself from outside. Here I am, in a foreign country, naked in a bathtub with a stranger who's masturbating in front of me. He could be anyone. The thought makes me explosively wet.

I can feel myself close to coming; my body's becoming heavy under the water and it's becoming more difficult to hold my head above the surface.

Suddenly you're standing right next to me. I look up and have your dick straight in front of me. Your jeans are now pulled down to your thighs together with your underwear, and you masturbate slowly. You don't take your eyes off me, maybe you can see how close I am. I feel the smell of you and your clothes, a slight sent of detergent and men's perfume mixed with the smell of dick. Your breathing is heavy and a slight red flush is beginning to show on your chest. The steam from the water must be making you warm.

I allow myself to close my eyes and feel the orgasm come. The water reaches my ears and I'm enfolded in a vacuum of silence. Your hand breaks the surface of the water and places itself safely under my head as support, and I come. I come so hard that I'm screaming, wildly. I feel the warmth of your breath near my cheek, your stubble caresses my face and I feel your smell even stronger. For a few seconds I feel almost euphoric, then the familiar heavy, comfortable feeling spreads through my body.

I look up at you. Your hand remains behind my neck. My

heart is beating strong and my pussy's pounding slowly. Small beads of sweat trickle down my hairline, the air in the bathroom is heavy with moist.

I rise to my knees slowly in the bathtub, the water runs off me and the cool air is fresh. You stand up again and I have your dick right in front of my mouth.

I don't think you could get any harder.

Pretty, fat dick.

I place both hands on the edge of the tub to support myself. I open my mouth wide and am able to fit almost your whole dick in my mouth. You inhale deeply and throw your head back.

You taste good, like warm skin and salt.

I suck you slowly and softly. When I have your whole dick in my mouth I press it against my throat and let it stay there for a few seconds. You hold your breath and I can feel your gaze above me. Sometimes it's more satisfying for me to give pleasure like this than to be the one to receive. It feels as if I'm in power of your body. My warm mouth could control you completely.

I pull back and look at you; you seem to be in your own world of pleasure. Right where I want you to be. I reach for the small bottle of lavender oil next to me. I pull the cork out with my teeth and smell it; a sweet smell of citrus and lavender.

I grab you by the hips and pull you closer so that your dick is above the tub. I fold my hand under your dick and pour the oil on top of it. I don't need to look up at you, I can hear you smiling.

I begin to rub your dick with both hands, first slowly and softly but then harder. I let one hand stay on your dick while I caress your scrotum with the other. Your breathing is heavy now.

I let my hand glide further in behind your scrotum and search for your ass. The oil makes it easy for me to glide my finger inside you. Your body twitches and I look up at you swiftly, you look surprised; your mouth open and your eyes clear. Two short moans and you come. I manage to direct your dick towards my breast, so that you cover them with your sperm.

When you've pulled your clothes off and wrapped my most scruffy towel around your thin hips you sit down on the toilet seat again and light a cigarette. You won't stop looking at me, but you're smiling in a completely different way now. From the bathtub I gesture for you to give me a cigarette as well, and you hand me the one you've just lit.

I look out through the gap in the blinds. It's going to be a warm day.

the reward

Sayo Coimbra

When I've been good you give me a reward. You lie down on your stomach across my lap. Your soft ass in my hands, the dimples on your butt cheeks, the small beauty mark which shines like a white spot. Someone spilled milk there, I said the first time I saw it. I licked the spot tenderly.

The reward tonight is that I'm allowed to do whatever I want with your body, with you laying there, your soft belly pressed against my thighs. You always tease me by moving your legs so that your butt quivers. I can almost hear you smile. Your skin smells of warmth, sweat and cigarettes. It's the best smell, better than any drug.

I don't know where to start - I never do - but I caress you gently with both hands. I massage your butt cheeks, restraining myself from biting down into them. I don't think I could bite gently, I would take a real bite.

I draw my fingers along your crack, just a light touch. I feel the tips of my fingers touch your ass, then your pussy. You're not wet yet. I know you'll get wet as soon as I start stroking your clitoris, but I make you wait. You don't have any patience at all when you're horny. You want everything at once; if I tease you too much you get angry.

I spread your legs a little more for a better angle, you make an approving sound, a prolonged *mmm* coming from somewhere between the curly strands of hair that have fallen across your face. I lift the curls away, placing them behind your ear. I need to see your face when you come.

I lick my one hand, the tips of the fingers, and press them gently against your clitoris. Moving them in small circles, I watch your face for a reaction. You close your eyes, concentrating on the movements that I make. I lean down and kiss your one cheek while I continue caressing you, my breasts pressed against your back, I hear your breathing slowing down. I press my hand more firmly against you, feeling how the wetness from your pussy mixes with the saliva from my fingers. You begin to move your hips, I feel you becoming more relaxed and your body heavier against mine. Your smell mixes with the smell of your pussy, it smells like sex. It smells like you.

With my free hand I grab you below your jaw. I continue to caress you while I pull you closer to me. You know what I want. You open your eyes and look at me. Light brown eyes with a dash of gold, your gaze piercing and full of desire. I bring my thumb up to your lips. You open your mouth and I let my thumb stroke your tongue. You know what I'm about to do and we both know that you'll come almost immediately.

I bring my hand down and press my thumb against your ass. Almost immediately I feel your pussy begin to swell against my other hand. You moan softy, hungrily, and I begin to touch you faster, increasing the pressure of my thumb. You begin to move your body as if you can't be still. You react exactly the same way each time, I'll never get tired of it.

You arch your back and press your whole lower body against my hands. I grab you firmly. You whimper and mumble, *more*, *more*. You keep looking at me but your gaze is cloudy now, your eyelids heavy. Your mouth is half-open.

You're almost on your knees now, thrusting against my strained hands. It becomes harder to follow you in your excitement; I brace myself against the bed and try my best. I begin to gasp, having you like this turns me on so much. Normally so collected and calm, you let go completely now. I love that my hands are making you behave like this.

My thumb glides into your ass slightly, your muscles flexing beneath your soft skin. I feel your entire body tensing and the orgasm approaching. You moan and the pace of your breathing increases, it sounds as if you're panting in between the moaning. I feel your entire body contracting. You almost manage to kick me, as one of your knees jerks up uncontrollably. I keep going and look at you. *Come*, I tell you, *come*. And you come.

You press against my fingers as hard as you can, I feel your ass contracting around my finger. Your moaning becomes a prolonged *ahhhhh*. You close your eyes when you come, grimace and press your face into the mattress.

You press your legs together. It becomes impossible for me to continue moving my hand. You always become oversensitive as soon as you've come. You remain in that position for a moment. Half your body lying across the bed, your ass up, with my hand jammed between your legs. You need a few seconds, I know.

Baby, lie down on your back, I say.

You flop over on your back and I'm able to remove my hand. You look at me and smile, with marks from the mattress covering your cheek.

the sex club

MALIN EDHOLM

What am I doing here? This scene could have easily been taken from a documentary about the opium dens of the Victorian era, an illegal burlesque club during prohibition, or a cabaret in the spirit of Moulin Rouge. It's a dark space, filled with cocktails, smoke and naked bodies.

I get a tingling sensation in my stomach. I've read about sex clubs before but I've never actually been to one. I can feel the hairs on my arms rising and my heart pounding hard in my chest.

At the door, we're greeted by a tall gangly individual, dressed only in glitter and a piece of clothing that covers the most sensitive part of the sex. Their body is coated with oil; their naked butt glimmering in pink. They offer a secretive smile when we arrive and tell us, in a honeyed voice.

"Hey darlings, so I'll tell you what you need to know: there are lockers right behind here where you can put your stuff and your clothes, if you want to undress. No pressure though. There's a big dance floor with a DJ further in, there's also a photographer on stage if you feel like getting a sexy picture taken. There are two more floors apart from this one, where you'll find rooms with different degrees of privacy. There are also tools, toys and protection for you both! Okay? Go play now!"

We let ourselves be gently prodded into the club, exchanging shy smiles and fumbling after each others' hands. This is our second date. The first date was casual; we got chai lattes in the sun and strolled along the seawall, taking turns talking about our lives. Among biking tourists, joggers and dog walkers she told me about her career, her two kids and her husband of 20 years. I told me about my day jobs, my travels and about Sweden.

In the club we put our valuables in lockers but keep our dresses on. The dance floor is full of people in different outfits and various states of nakedness. It's dark and teeming with glitter, feathers and leather. Uninhibited, people are dancing without shirts, without pants, without bras. In this sea of bodies, all different shapes and sizes, everyone is allowed to join in. The air is heavy with anticipation and sex.

After a couple of cocktails and a few songs later we brush against each other lightly. I feel a rush bubble up inside me. She's so sexy dancing in front of me like that. Her green dress hugs her soft body and generous hips. She's much cooler than me with her tattooed arms and purple hair, I know it. But her glittering eyes tell me something else entirely when they devour me amidst the fog from the smoke machine.

One of my favorite songs starts to play; a song that always makes me move my hips a little extra. I feel horny and sexy. In my head a scene from the movie Flashdance begins to play; I know I probably look nothing at all like Alex, but the feeling is tickling. My date smiles at me and rewards my eager dancing with a small applaud.

An impulse grabs hold of me and I reach up and release the halterneck tie of my dress, letting it fall to the floor. I move in closer to her body and she meets me halfway with her mouth. She tastes of alcohol and mint. Her tongue quickly finds its way into my mouth and I can feel a tingle spread through my entire body. Her mouth is cool from the drink but the movement of our tongues quickly creates heat.

We are surrounded by dancing people. Naked people. People wearing all kinds of outfits. Horny people. People in love. Happy people. I feel safe. I feel euphoric.

I run my hands up and down her body and we begin to move our hips against each other. Melting into each other, our hands become increasingly secure and every caress feels more and more intense.

She takes my hand and leads me up to the second floor. On the way we pass couples and groups of people in all kinds of intimate positions. Instinctively, I look away, not wanting to disturb them. Some of them wave at us and ask if we would like to join, to come play with them, but we keep going.

We pass a room where I can see a beautiful woman lying down in a sex swing. My gaze follows the curve of her body; she's interlocked with another woman through a double dildo.

The dildo penetrates them both to the rhythm of the swing. A third person stands behind them, repeatedly teasing their bodies with a soft whip. Their moaning awakens an erotic curiosity in me. My whole body hums with kinetic potential and my sex feels heavy and wet. I hesitate, temped to remain and observe, but am too absorbed by my thoughts of her; of being alone with her, without others and without toys. At least to begin with.

We enter a room with four beds, they all have curtains around them, allowing complete privacy. The mattress is shiny and easy to wipe off, like the high school gym wrestling mat. At the top of the bed fresh towels, lube, condoms, antibacterial gel and candy are neatly arranged.

"You want me to close the drapes, hun?"

The affectionate term makes me blush, but I remind myself that this is a cultural difference; a stock phrase and that she doesn't mean anything by it. This isn't a complicated romantic relationship, we're only here to enjoy each others' company and touch.

"Yes please."

My voice sounds slightly nervous. I don't know exactly how I feel about the thought of anyone seeing us having sex. It's both exhilarating and embarrassing.

We close the drapes almost all the way, leaving only the slightest gap. It's thrilling. The scent of lust hangs in the air, a tangible sweetness.

I fondle her long leg while removing her stay ups, caressing her foot through the thin nylon. I take my time and let my fingers lazily stroke her body, all her curves and dimples. A tremble moves through her, making the hair on her body rise. Her skin, covered in goosebumps, feels warm under my fingers.

Mimicking my motions, she slowly removes my bra, stopping to admire my stiff nipples, to pinch and pull them just a little. My body tenses from the touch and my breasts tighten.

She lets the tip of her tongue wiggle and circle around one of my hard, raw nipples and folds it into her mouth, sucking on it, then adding teeth – at first gently and then more aggressively. I begin to breathe heavier, stroking her thighs and butt more firmly, digging my nails into her skin, making her moan.

Encouraged, I follow the inside of her thighs with my mouth, all the way up to her swollen lips. I bend down and start licking. My tongue moves over her folds, her opening; it's salty and soft. I focus on her opening, letting my tongue play along the edge, entering her slightly.

Her moaning and whimpering makes me want to keep teasing her. I reach up with the tip of my tongue and play with her clitoris. I feel her wetness against my chin, she grabs the back of my neck and presses herself harder against me. I begin to lick her more eagerly.

Switching positions, I lie down under her, careful not to let my face become seperated from her pussy. She relaxes and eases herself down onto my face, filling my mouth with her lips, her wetness, her heat. I open my mouth and welcome her sex, craving everything at once.

I feel her hand stroking my thigh, finding its way into my wet panties. She plays with my pubic hair, twining my curls between her fingers before caressing my swollen lips gently. Slowly, she lets the tip of one of her fingers find its way inside my vagina.

While my tongue plays with her clit, her wrist massages the upper part of my sex. She pulls the hood of my clitoris rhytmically as if she is jerking me off.

Her whimpering reaches a higher pitch as I press my face closer to her body. My nose is trapped inside her pussy and all my senses are filled with her. She smells sweet and bitter at the same time and I kiss her roughly. Her hips rock against me and I can feel her becoming tighter and tighter until, finally, her sex contracts in spasms, pulsating at an even pace.

Her climax is heavy and comes straight at me, her fluids running into my mouth while her pussy keeps humming against my lips.

At the same time, her fingers continue to move inside me. It's as if it's her own body she's stroking, as if she's known my body her whole life. Her hands are everywhere, caressing, pulling, pinching, pushing, rubbing. I bite her earlobe in lust and frustration, feeling the unmistakable sensation of the orgasm approaching. It's an addiction, a desire and force that I have no control over.

My legs begin to shake, I almost pull away from her persistent touch, but she holds me down, pushing my legs apart, keeping me exposed to her fingers and her tongue. I don't know where to go and her determined hands give me no choice. My whole body is screaming, tingling and flexing.

Looking up, I see someone gazing right at me – a pair of eyes glimmering in the gap of the curtain. They look hungry.

When I finally climax, it is with my eyes interlocked with the stranger's eyes. When my body finally relaxes, I close my eyes momentarily.

When I open my eyes again the stranger is gone and the relief I felt short-lived. My lust like a growing itch.

I grab my partner by the hips and turn her over, gesturing for her to get on all fours. I get on my knees as well, standing behind her with my pelvic bone pressing against her soft butt. I rub my sex against her, the movement massaging us both. Reaching across her body, my hand easily finds its way to her wet opening once more.

This time I decide to explore her with my fingers. I let my fingers slide inside her and feel her softness. I feel her deepen and widen as I insert more fingers, and my movements become firmer and more demanding. Her skin is like silk under my fingers, smooth and soft.

Slowly, I can feel her tighten around my fingers. The contractions reverberate through my body. She moans uncontrollably and falls forward softly on the mattress. I wait to remove my hand, enjoying the feeling of being enveloped by her flesh.

For a few minutes we just lie there, breathing heavily into each others' mouths. She strokes my body, caressing and drawing little circles with her fingers, before climbing on top of me. Grabbing hold of my hands, she pins them down over my head and rubs her swollen, wet sex against mine. Excitement grips me and I struggle with desire, the desire to be liberated.

I want to place my hands on her soft body, to be filled by her once more, but she holds me down. Our pussies meet and press against each other, I tighten my butt and thrust up against her.

Her tongue, wet and heavy, finds my ear. It tickles my whole body and makes me shudder. She's whispering.

"I'm gonna make you come so many times you won't be able to stand up once I'm done."

Her voice is raspy and playful. I caress her neck with my teeth, resisting the temptation to bite down hard. I lick and kiss her throat and collarbone while she fucks me hard. The feeling of her weight is overwhelming, all I can think of is wanting her more, wanting her harder.

With every movement that brings our bodies together, the orgasm builds in my body, making all the muscles throb. The spasms start deep inside me, at my core, and I let them rise until the swelling moves unhindered through my body. Her climax is the mirror image of mine, and we greedily lock mouths and breath together. Her nails on my skin draw blood, but I can't feel it.

We sink down on the mattress and embrace each other in mutual whimpering, sometimes moaning with sheer enjoyment. The juice from her pussy is on my lips and in my mouth, mine is in hers. Yet, we don't stop for long, we continue to devour each others' bodies feverishly; to search for new ways to come and enjoy each other.

A few hours later, when we once again sink back on to the mattress, our sweaty bodies melt together. I have a strong sensation that our bodies have become one; I can no longer tell which limbs are hers and which are mine. I see amusement in her eyes when she smiles at me, indulgence almost. My cheeks are hot and I'm suddenly aware of how red my face must appear. I blush even more at the thought that this is making me self-conscious, after everything we've done together.

I let my mind drift away, letting it hover over the bed and gaze at myself from above, gaze at us. The image of our knot of bodies is deeply peaceful.

Later, when we kiss each other good night, we are both dizzy and tired. Tomorrow, I'll return home to Sweden. I'm struck by the realization that we'll most likely never meet again. All that will remain of our evening here together will be the memory; the happy memory of the sex club in Mount Pleasant.

summer night

SAGA BECKER

Tick, tick, tick, tick. I shake the bottle. The sound of the little lead bullet, helping to distribute the paint evenly, calms me down. Givs me something to focus on. Keeps my nerves in check. The darkness is almost complete now. I rely on my gut feeling; gut feeling and muscle memory. After all, the sketch I made is only small-scale, applying it is something else. This is where it goes from thought to reality.

We've painted trains on and off since we were seventeen. We're twenty-four now. It's a game, a contest. It's a sport. It's also so much more. It's part of who I am. You've got to be quick and fully focused. There is no room for hesitation. When you start hesitating, that's when things can go bad. Sometimes we find legal spots to paint, designated walls and stuff like that, but it's never the same. There's no adrenaline to it, and there's definitely not the rush of seeing a brand-new train roll into the platform with your tag on it.

Not that it ever stays there for long, sure, but long enough to catch the attention of the right kind of people. And believe me, they talk about us. They talk about the risks we take, how we challenge others and ourselves. How we push each other in the right direction without being too reckless or hotheaded. This, tonight, is our biggest challenge so far. An entirely new wagon, set to be inaugurated first thing tomorrow morning. We knew from the start it wasn't going to be easy. They've upped the security around this train. Still, here we are, cans in hand.

We're a good team. You have to give us that. Josef, Elias and myself. We complement each other. Elias with his comical figures and satirical approach, Josef's graphic, minimal designs, and my own abstract, floating style. It's an unexpected mix. It's fresh. We started out with workshops at the youth center, finding legal walls, advancing up to abandoned buildings and warehouses, until we finally started roaming the entire city. There're still some spots left here and there with our very first tags. In the last few years we've calmed down a bit though. These days the things we do is more advanced, less driven by excess energy and more by the desire to create.

"Cassandra! You need to finish up, they'll be coming any minute now!"

Josef smiles at me with his warm, brown eyes.

"I'm almost done."

I turn my head towards him, smile reassuringly, and continue to paint.

I've never been one of those girly girls. I've always wanted to do the same stuff as the guys. Climb trees, play soccer, learn to skate. That's how I got to know Josef and Elias. I came to their school when I was eleven, and they welcomed me with open arms. I quickly became one of the gang. We've been together ever since. Pretty simple when you think about it. We were three outsiders who found security in each other's company. Together we became less weird, or at least as weird. That's how everyone else labelled us; just plain weird. Not that we really cared, as long as we were together. We found our own community, our own spaces. We made each other grow, with the help of skate boards and spray cans. With them I felt less wrong. With Josef and Elias I feel right.

"Cassandra! Let's go!" Josef's voice is urgent now.

"I'm just gonna finish this last part."

Josef shakes his head, laughing at the same time. He knows that I know what I'm doing. I pick up a new spray can

– black. I'd never let us leave without our imprint. Even if people recognize our style I want them to never forget our name. I could paint it in my sleep. It's second nature. I draw the lines quickly and back away to have a look. I drop the can. Elias comes up behind me and snaps a photo. I pull my hoodie up over my head, shoulder my backpack and jam the skateboard under my arm. The three of us look at each other, nodding affirmatively, smiling. Then we run like hell.

It doesn't take long for the guards to appear. I hear their heavy steps behind us, the beams of their flashlights lighting up the path ahead. I feel the familiar surge of adrenaline, the moment when the body takes over completely, the instinct to survive. Suddenly in front of us a guard appears with a dog. The german shepherd barks aggressively, baring its gums.

My heart is beating. Fuck, they're gaining on us. Elias manages to squeeze past the guard with the dog, attracting its attention, so that Josef and I can slip by. We run across the subway tracks as fast as we can. We've got this. We know exactly how to run, where to split up, when to shake them off.

Adrenaline pumps hard through my body, my pulse is high. I feel alive. Nothing else compares to this feeling, it's unique. I stop and pause behind a brick wall, the blood beating in my temples. I look up at the dark starry sky and it feels like the whole world is at my feet. A warm, soothing feeling fills my stomach. My insides fill with strength, the sudden sensation of belonging, of being invincible. I am unbreakable. Damn, I live for these moments.

"Do you really know where we're going?" I ask, while catching the branch that Elias lets go in front me.

"Yes, yes, yes… I'm a hundred percent sure," he says and plods on through the branches. After making sure we were clear of the guards we shared a few beers and Elias got the brilliant idea that we should go swimming, claiming he knew a great spot. As we make our way through a grove of trees, I sneak a peek at Josef. Walking next to me, he rolls his eyes and we start laughing.

Elias is the most impulsive of the three of us; always down for anything and never saying no to a challenge or adventure. Also, he never shuts up. He is probably the most extroverted of our group. He's also the one who's carried the most internalized anger against the world, but that's become better with age. You never know what is going to happen when you're with Elias, but you know it's going to be fun.

Josef can, at first, seem reserved, even shy; the calmest and most self-assured of us three. He's got a lot of integrity and doesn't seem to feel like he's got anything to prove, unlike Elias. Josef doesn't waste breath, making everything he says seem important. He is also the most considerate of us, always weighing the risks and very meticulous in his planning. I'm probably a mix of both, as impulsive as Elias but also cautious like Josef. We complement each other well.

I can't remember a night this hot. It's well after midnight but the temperature is still above twenty-five degrees celsius. My clothes stick to my body like an extra layer of skin I just want to rip off.

"Come on!" Elias' voice comes from far into the woods in front of us. There's an impatient note in his voice.

Josef pushes me forward playfully and I almost drop my skateboard. He grins and runs along ahead. There's something about Josef tonight, something different. I can't really put my finger on it. He feels impatient and more spontaneous than usual. There's something with Elias too, something even more impatient than how he normally is. Branches scrape against my bare legs. It's hard to see anything among the trees. I rely on my hearing, following the sounds of the boys in front of me. Gradually, a clear blue light appears.

"Ha! What did I tell you?"

Elias spreads his arms and points to the cut-out hole in the fence. We laugh at him. Ahead of us there's a big lawn; a little further, a large, illuminated swimming pool.

"What do you say? Ready for a swim?"

Elias bends the hole in the fence open wider and throws his board and backpack through, waiting for us to move forward.

"Watch out for the edges, they're sharp." Josef lays his hand on the small of my back, guiding me forward. The feeling of his hot hand sends a warm tingling sensation through my body, straight to my pulsating sex.

I don't know what's going on tonight. There's something in the air. It's been like this the whole day, the whole night. It's not just me. I can feel it in Josef. I can feel it in Elias. I think they can feel it in me too. I don't know if it's the alcohol, the sudden heat, or the company. Maybe it's a combination of all three. We've known each other forever and we've hung out almost every day this summer. Pretty much all our adolescense actually. Why would tonight be any different?

Josef climbs through the fence after me, squats down, opens his backpack and brings out three beers. He opens the first beer, spraying foam everywhere. With his eyes on Elias, who just came through the fence behind us, he licks the foam away from the top of the can.

I watch how Elias pulls his hand through his messy blond hair, avoiding eye contact but smiling. I can see it at the corners of his mouth, how they sort of twitch upwards, making my sex unexpectedly twitch too. Elias accepts the beer from Josef, adjusts his pants over his groin, then runs across the lawn. Josef cracks open another beer and hands it to me, before opening a can for himself.

"Cheers," he says, holding out his can of beer while gazing into my eyes. We toast and he tilts his head backwards. The movement makes his hoodie slide off his head, exposing his cropped hair. I watch his Adam's apple as it bobs up and down while he swallows, big gulps, beer trickling down the corners of his mouth and down his neck. Laughing, he brings his arm up and uses his sleeve to wipe his face.

We run across the lawn, towards the glowing water. Everything else is dark. Elias is already standing by the edge of the pool, he downs his beer, tosses the can on the ground, kicks of his shoes, pulls off his t-shirt and looks back at us. He pulls his shorts down, along with his underwear, baring his pale bum as dives into the water soundlessly. Surfacing, he shakes his curly blonde hair.

"Fuck, this is sweet!" He's floating on his back, shouting up towards the sky. Josef removes the speakers from his backpack and connects them to his phone. Soon, the sound of hiphop reverberates through the night. I kick off my sneakers while pulling off my hoodie. The bun on top of my head comes loose and my hair falls down over my face. I let it flow free. I unbutton my shorts, take my socks off and collect everything in a small pile. I release the knot of my bikini, pull it over my head and throw it on the pile.

I'm very happy with my body; skating keeps me in shape. My boobs are small. Without makeup, if I'm wearing a cap or hoodie, people often mistake me for a boy. I'm still very satisfied with my boobs and no one has ever said anything negative about them.

I decide to keep my panties on, wondering when last I shaved. About two or three days ago, it should be fine. Not that it matters really, but I keep them on anyway.

I look over at Josef who is busy getting out of his shorts and boxers. His hand reaches up over his clean-shaven head, then moves down his chest and belly. Beneath his belly button there's a strand of dark hair trailing down to his sex, his darkness. He's got a fantastic body. Long lean muscles moving under the skin.

Josef looks over at Elias in the water, pausing as he catches me staring at him. I look away, feeling my face flush – it burns. When I dare look back at him again he holds my gaze, looking at me with a serious expression. He raises one eyebrow, then grins, shakes his head, and dives in.

A tremble passes through my body and I feel my nipples stiffen. I pull my hand through my hair, using it to cover my boobs before carefully walking over to the edge of the pool.

"Let's go, chicken!" Elias yells and dives down below the

surface, pressing his pale butt upwards. He chokes on his own laughter. Sitting on the edge I dip my feet in the cool water. Elias and Josef start splashing water at each other. Suddently, Josef catches hold of Elias, pushing him down under the surface. Elias comes up laughing and sputtering, pretending to be angry and trying to get back at Josef.

They play-fight, taking turns keeping the other one locked under the water. Surfacing at the same time, they suddenly stop. Their eyes meet and neither of them look away. They are dangerously close. Breathing heavy, Elias bites down on his lower lip, finally averting his eyes. Elias, usually so brave and confident, suddenly look insecure and, in a way, vulnerable. He dives below the surface again and swims away. Josef looks over at me and smiles before flopping over on his back. Josef, Josef – what are you up to? What are you doing with Elias? What are you doing with me?

I push my body away from the edge of the pool and let myself sink down into the water, until every part of my body is below the surface. In the water the sounds become muffled. My body feels light and loose. With circular movements, I make myself go deeper.

The music echoes from above and my warm body is one with the water. Feeling the need of oxygen, I push off, back up to the surface. Floating on my back, breathing heavy, I look up at the sky. Elias and Josef swim up to the edge next to where I'm floating. I lay one arm around Josef and the other around Elias, letting them keep my body afloat. Our bodies are slippery and soft against each other.

"We really took it next level tonight," Josef says.

"Are you kidding," Elias says. "I can't wait to see everyone's reactions tomorrow!"

Josef grins, fills his mouth with water and sprays it over us. We all laugh.

"You know what?" I say. "You two are the best people in my life. I don't know what I would do without you."

I turn my head and kiss Elias on the cheek. When I turn around to do the same with Josef he kisses me on the mouth. My first reaction is to laugh and I notice that Elias is laughing too. Josef, though, isn't laughing. He looks at me calmly with his glowing brown eyes. He reaches forward and kisses me again. This time, I kiss him back. His tongue is soft and heavy. The stubble around his mouth scratches me pleasantly. Pulling away from his lips, I breathe heavy. Josef smiles, looking over at Elias.

I turn my eyes to Elias who is also serious now. I slowly bend toward him. He bends toward me. I kiss him. He kisses me back. His tongue is also soft but not as confident, more hesitant and curious. While we kiss I feel Josef's hand caressing my back. Feeling my pulse rise, I shiver with pleasure. My whole body tingles when we stop kissing. I look back at Elias and then at Josef. They press their bodies closer against me. Josef, with his dark eyes, looks straight at Elias. He's breathing is heavy, it's as if he's not sure of where to go.

I've never seen Elias this vulnerable and open before. It is incredibly exciting to see Josef, who's normally the quiet one, take the initiative and commando. He leans forward slowly. I think we all have the feeling that this is it, it's now or never. Elias leans in, and their lips meet. They kiss. I caress their backs. The kiss deepens, getting harder, making them breathe heavier. I wonder if their pulse is beating as fast as mine, if their hearts are beating as hard as mine. It beats uncontrollably, and I shiver. They boys stop kissing and Josef's eyes glimmer. He looks at Elias and then back at me.

"Are you both okay?" he asks.

I look at Elias, and then back at Josef. I nod my head slowly and we both look over at Elias who is also nodding. Josef can't contain his smile, it's all over his face. His dimples would make anyone melt. He kisses Elias, and then me again. He looks up at the grass, giving us a questioning look. We confirm. Heaving himself up out of the pool, he turns around and sits down on the edge – looking down on his hard cock laying against his belly. He smiles shyly and reaches down towards Elias, helping him up.

Elias dick is also hard; it's slimmer but longer compared to Josef's. When they kiss, I wish I could save the image in my mind forever.

They both extend their hands, lifting me up out of the

water. I am weightless in the darkness, I feel so small in their arms, so pliable. So soft against their hardness. New feelings well up inside of me. They're so beautiful. I take my time to smell each of them. First Josef and then Elias. Even if I already know how they smell, I've never experienced them like this before. They smell like they always do; safe, comforting smells, but mixed in are also completely new fragrances.

We move over to the lawn. The excitement of discovering someone else's body for the first time is overwhelming. Their smell, their taste. Every person has their unique fragrance, their unique taste. To explore a new person is one of the most erotic things I know.

I end up standing between Josef and Elias with their hands all over me, soft, caressing. I feel their hands tremble with nervousness and excitement. I take one cock in each hand and stroke them both at the same time, carefully. The both lean down and kiss my neck.

I see that both of their cocks are glimmering with pre-cum. I bring their dicks towards each other, letting them meet. Their juices mix, slippery against one another. They both breathe down into my hair. I notice that they don't really seem to know what to do with their hands, which sweetly fumble over my body. I can see how much they want to be near one another but seem afraid to be the one to take the first step.

"Kiss each other." I whisper, and they do as I say.

They are unbelievably beautiful. I trail a line of kisses down both of their chests and stomachs, until I am on my knees in front of them. I let my fingers stroke their cocks, caressing them, jerking them off. I take Elias cock and bring it to my mouth. It tastes sweet and salty at the same time. I swallow it as deep as I can, almost down to its root. Elias moans into Josef's mouth.

Biting my lip, I innocently look up at them both. I then take Josef in my mouth. He's thicker and harder to fit, tastes different but still the same. They interlock their fingers, continuing to kiss while their free hands loose themselves in my hair. I take turns with their dicks in my mouth, letting them rub against each other. Rubbing their wet tips together.

My sex is throbbing, like it's on fire, whenever they look at me. They've never looked at me like this before. They look at me now as if they're seeing me in a completely different way, and I feel it right down to my gut.

"You are so beautiful," Josef mumbles, gazing into my eyes. His voice is dark and raspy. It scratches me from the inside. It occurs to me that I've never heard him say anything like that before, not to anyone. He's dated people and had partners before but I've never heard him give actual compliments. It's a different Josef that is being exposed to Elias and I tonight.

"You're both so wonderful. The most beautiful people I know."

He smiles, embarrassed, like he just realized what he's said. I know what he's saying is real. Josef doesn't play games, is never false. I look at Elias, who's uncharacteristically quiet. I don't think I've ever heard him be silent for this long before. Both Josef and I know that he is the least experienced of the three of us when it comes to sex. He's talked about it before; how unsure he feels, how afraid he is of doing something wrong, of not knowing what to do. Standing there, he blushes and looks a little lost. I can see how rigid his body is, how tense his muscles are beneath his skin, how he's pretending to seem relaxed. He's quiet, apprehensive, his face thoughtful.

I pull them both down to their knees beside me. Guiding them towards me, showing them with my whole body that this is about all three of us, that we are here together. We all kiss. Elias more carefully than Josef. He's exploring. He's watching, feeling and smelling. It's beautiful to see him gradually relax.

Our tongues stroke one another. Josef takes Elias's cock with one hand, moving his hand gently up and down.

Elias bites his lip, smiling nervously. I can see him glancing down at Josef's crotch curiously. I can tell he wants to, but is too afraid. I take his hand and carefully bring it down to Josef's cock. They masturbate each other while I take turns kissing them.

We fall back on the grass, me in the middle and them on both sides of me. I've never felt so beautiful before, so sexy, so light. Their hands are all over me, all over my body. Pinching, pulling and scratching. My pussy's pounding and a shiver runs through me. The boys find their way to my breasts, taking a nipple each in their mouths, without losing eye contact with each other. I breathe heavy, pushing my lower body up and down against the grass. The grass is smooth and wet against my back, thighs and feet.

With his fingers Josef plays with the edge of my panties, looking at me with a question mark in his eyes. I nod and he pulls them off. Elias licks my left breast while Josef circles the brown spots on my belly with his tongue. He's moving downward, letting his tongue trace my body; kissing, licking, caressing. I put my hand on his shaven head and gently press him further down. He circles his pointy tongue around my lower belly, kissing the inside of my thighs while spreading my legs with his big arms. He flattens his tongue out and licks in between my legs.

I moan loudly and sink my fingers into Elias' curly hair. The feeling on Josef's soft tongue makes me spread my legs wider. Elias gently bites my nipple with his lips, before sucking on it. He smiles, his blue eyes gleaming. He lets go of my nipple, gets on his knees in front of me and pulls his cock up and down in front of my face. I notice how he's become more relaxed and comfortable in his body, which makes me incredibly horny.

I love how he looks down at his cock almost with pride, while jerking it off. I run my tongue across my lips, bite my lower lip and look and him affirmatively. He guides his cock to my mouth and I open, letting him enter. Carefully, he grabs my neck, twining his fingers into my hair. I grab his buttocks with one hand on each cheek, forcing him to push himself deeper into my mouth. I help him find a rhythm to fuck my throat. He steadies himself in the grass above me, while pushing himself into me. Josef keeps licking me with a deep, lazy tongue. He sucks on my clit, massaging it slowly with the tip of his tongue. Gently he pushes two fingers inside me, I'm so wet they glide in easy. Carefully he wriggles them around inside me, before taking them out and bringing them to his mouth.

"You taste sweet."

I hear him whisper. He dives back in with his fingers. It's so wonderful to feel his fingers inside me, stretching me, exploring me. Taking them out once more, he reaches over to Elias this time, who grips Josef's hands and suck his fingers. The sight of them makes my whole body burn, igniting me from the inside.

Josef lays down on his back, clearly showing me that he wants me to sit on his face. Elias pulls me up and moves me forward, helping me lift my leg up to mount Josef's face. As soon as I sit down, Josef buries his face in my crotch, extending his tongue and sucking my whole clit into his mouth. I can't control my moaning, the sounds escape me and I lose my balance.

Elias is quick, catching me as I fall back, he helps me to regain my balance and rhythm. I ride Josef's face. Elias caresses his cock, looking pensive. He bends down and whispers something in Josef's ear, who continues to fuck me with his tongue, in long heavy strokes.

I close my eyes, disappear into myself. Josef spreads my lips and lets his tongue find its way inside me wile rubbing my clit between his fingers. Suddenly he stops and blows hot, heavy air straight at my sex.

I open my eyes and see Elias, laying on his side, right next to Josef. With curious eyes, he licks the shaft of Josef's cock. Then, closing his eyes, he takes Josef in his mouth. I see his expression change, a tranquil feeling taking hold of his features. Its as if he's found home, something longed for. At the same time he's stroking his own dick with determined movements. Josef's moaning straight into my pussy. I keep riding his face, letting his tongue glide in and out of me. I pinch my own nipples, rolling them between my thumb and index finger as I enjoy the sight of Elias pressing Josef into his mouth.

Usually I would never dare to do what we are now doing. But I feel so safe with them. So safe and free, and I notice they feel the same. They take, they give. It is astonishingly exciting and their moaning moves my soul, making me extremely horny.

With my one hand, I show Josef how to touch my clit and lick me at the same time. He follows my lead and I feel how close I am to coming, my climax only a few moments away. This surprises me. I've never been able to come with anyone else before. A lot of times because I haven't dared to show the other person how I want to be touched, wanted them to touch me. Show them my desires.

With Josef and Elias things are different. Of course there's nervousness, we've never done this before. But I don't feel scared of being judged by them. I pretty sure they feel the same way.

"I'm gonna come soon."

Josef voice is like a growl, making Elias smile happily. Straddling Josef's leg, he puts his own cock on top of Josef's, letting the two cocks glide over each other. He takes his dick between his thumb and index finger, pushing out pre-cum with which he strokes both their tips with. Then, taking both cocks in one hand, he jerks them off at the same time.

I press myself down further against Josef's face while he rubs my clit harder. I've found a rhythm that works and

I begin to breathe heavier and harder. I tighten my thighs. Tighten my pelvis. Pushing it back and forth, tightening my pussy. I'm so close. Instinctively, I reach down and being to rub my clit. Josef makes room for my fingers, his tongue still playing inside me. Closing my eyes, all sound disappears. It feels as if I'm under water again, weightless. At the same time, it's as if I've never been this heavy before.

I climax all over Josef's face. Everything is black. I fall to the side, laying back down in the grass. My whole body shakes, I feel it shuddering and sending out burning electricity from my sex. It radiates.

When I open my eyes again I see Elias lying over Josef. Josef's stomach and chest is drenched in their sperm. Breathing heavy, they kiss each other. Josef twitches as Elias touches his cock, laughing. They grin into each other's mouths.

I crawl up against them, and they gently remove some strands of hair from my face. Our bodies smell of chlorine, skin and sex. It's a whole new mix of fragrances. Elias rolls off Josef and lays down on the grass. We lie close together, Josef in the middle with Elias and I on each side.

"You have no idea how many times I've fantasized about this and hoped that someday it might happen," he whispers to us.

"I would lie if I said I'd never thought about it either," I whisper.

"Yeah, the idea has struck me," Elias says, and we all crack up laughing.

Josef places a kiss on my forehead, then on Elias', before pulling us tighter against his chest. I look up at the starlit sky and it feels like the whole world is at our feet.

An entirely new feeling is growing inside of me. A curious strength fills my insides, a force that says that the three of us – who are pretty small in this big world – can become bigger together, that we can become something else, that we are invincible. We are unbreakable. I have found a new way to live, something new to live for, something new to live through.

pink desire

OTTILIA. E

She's immersed in her own bubble of joy and ecstasy. Dancing on her own, for herself, completely absorbed in the music. The heat and sweat brought on by hours of dancing is making her increasingly horny.

She leaves dance floor to find some water. Standing by the bar, unexpectedly, there he is. The guy with the jet black hair. She doesn't know a lot about him except that he seems sporty, always walking around with a gym bag, and listens to techno. And that he's not at all her type.

Sure, his body seems amazing; the muscles of his stomach perceptible through his loose fitting t-shirt. But the people she normally ends up going home with usually have something else about them; some quality or oddity that sparks her interest, promising that whatever happens between them will be worthwhile. If she were to summarize this guy with one word it would be ordinary. She almost gets bored just by looking at him.

They've worked together at the same office for about six months now, never exchanging more than the most mundane small talk in the corridor and lunch room. Making his way towards her through the crowd, she can tell he's eager to connect with her, and she toys with the notion of maybe trying to tease something more exciting out of him.

An hour and a half later, after a twenty minute ride on the subway's south going red line, they arrive at his apartment. Once inside she heads straight for the bedroom, gesturing for him to follow her. She pushes him down on the bed, pinning him down roughly, telling him to keep still. Gently, she caresses his entire body, enjoying the feeling of goose-bumps rising under her fingers. Now and then she pauses her stroking movements and spanks him, quick and hard. He moans, equally in shock and pleasure. She's already undressed him; he's naked except for his boxers and smells of soap and, more faintly, beer.

There's no mistaking the big bulge that's pressing against his tight blue boxers. The tip is already sticking out of his underwear, too hard to be contained. But she keeps on ignoring his rigid dick, even though the mere look at it makes her vagina swell in arousal. Her panties are heavy and wet from her soaked pussy.

She continues to slowly caress his body with her fingers, tongue and breasts, making sure to touch every inch of him.

Her tongue circles and plays with one of his hard nipples while her fingers pinch the other. Through clenched teeth he's breathing heavy, emitting growling sounds from deep down his throat. His nipples are now as hard as the dick she keeps ignoring.

She carefully licks the tip of his nipple before biting down into it, hard enough for his body to become rigid with anticipation. He lets go of a low moan. His hands glide up to touch her hips, continuing upwards to her heavy breasts that lie against his stomach. She lets his hands roam, enjoying the freedom of wearing only panties instead of all the usual layers. When she feels his fingers make their way inside her underway she removes his hands firmly, places them above his head and signals that she wants them to stay there. He nods affirmatively, she's the one in control, she's the one with power.

She straddles his belly, just above the sensitive, gleaming tip of the solid dick sticking out of his boxers. She can see desire swell in his eyes. He keeps his arms above his head while she bends down to lick his armpit. He tastes of sweat and sex, a sweet taste. She takes a deep breath before putting her mouth against his ear and letting her tongue lick all its crevices, as if to clean it, making him squirm beneath her.

She strokes his firm abs all the way down to his boxers, letting one finger glide alongside the hem, careful to avoid touching his cock.

Her wet sex sticks to his stomach and the only thing she can think about is slowly gliding her pussy down his dick. She wants to mount him gradually and feel his hard thickness inside her: feel him filling her completely and her holding him in her warm vagina.

Breathing heavy now into his ear she removes her panties. Instead of sliding down his belly to let his cock enter her she straddles his thigh. Her vagina leaves a wet trail as she rubs against his smooth leg.

When she reaches down and puts her hand inside his boxers to stroke him, he trembles but manages to lie still, keeping his arms above his head and eyes closed.

She alternates between massaging, pulling and stroking his dick. Moving her sex faster and faster against his thigh, she can feel the orgasm rise and build in her body.

Her vagina is pounding and her clit, sensitive and throbbing, feels like the center of the universe. When the orgasm hits her, she can feel her insides contract, the feeling so intense it makes it difficult to breathe. Finally, with a roar, she releases, letting the feeling spread through her trembling body. She loves the sensation of allowing her mind to go blank like this; her heart races and colored dots appear behind her closed eyelids.

She lets go of his dick and shifts her body so that she can use her teeth to fold his boxers down. Her lips touch his pulsating sex and she feels his dick become impossibly hard. She licks her lips and uses the tip of her tongue to glide down the smooth shaft. Needing to feel him completely naked, she reaches up and pulls off his boxers.

She spends a few seconds just looking at him, his naked body, his dark curls and smooth, slick muscles. Her thighs are wet and sticky from the orgasm but she can tell her body is ready for another one. Not yet though. First she's going to enjoy giving him the release she knows he's craving.

She turns him over onto his stomach and strokes his thigh all the way up to his butt. He shivers and the hair on his skin rises. She continues to stroke and massage his inner thigh, moving closer and closer to his balls and butt.

Bending over, she takes his balls in her mouth while pinching his butt cheeks. She spanks his round, tight butt, hearing him moan into the pillow. Her fingers leave a red mark on his skin.

She massages his cheeks with big motions, letting her fingers touch more and more of him. Slowly, she approaches his anus, feeling his quivering longing and excitement. She doesn't know if he's spreading his legs wider and pushing his butt towards her consciously or not, but it's obvious he wants more. She continues to massage the opening of his anus with her fingers, now and then spanking him and hearing the intake of breath through his teeth, mixed with sensual whimpers.

She's softening him up, letting his moaning and his longing calls make her horny again. When she finally enters him with the tip of her finger he emits a sharp and surprised groan. Carefully she moves her finger in and out, making circles inside him. When she enters him with another finger he gets up on all four, unable to lay still. He moves his body towards her fingers, meeting them. He bends his back and pushes his butt against her hand, enabling her to penetrate him deeply.

Pulling out slowly, she gets up from the bed. He looks back at her as she brings out the lube from her backpack. She enjoys his anticipating gaze as he watches her step into the harness and thread it up her hips. She places the pink slim dildo over her pelvic bone and looks down at it, feeling electrified. It still feels a bit strange seeing herself with a strap-on, she hasn't fully gotten used to the image of it yet.

But it's exhilarating, and a thrill of pleasure runs through her when she sees her own excitement mirrored in his eyes.

She assumes a wide stance behind him on the bed and he crawls backwards towards her. She pours lube generously over her hand, the sticky strawberry-scented liquid dripping from her fingers. She continues to stroke him rhythmically with her fingers. He trembles and moans until finally he pleadingly asks her to fuck him, to fuck him hard.

"Please, take me. Fuck me hard."

His whimpering makes it hard to hear what he's saying.

She spanks him and his body reacts immediately. His voice gets louder, more commanding.

"Fuck me, hard, now!"

She gives him what he wants. After applying more sticky lube on the pink dildo she slides it into his anus and starts thrusting into him. He adjusts his body to meet her movements while she takes a firm grip of his hips.

Together they find a rhythm where their bodies meet and are reduced to one sexual, sweaty creature. Every thrust into him caresses her, exciting her and making her thrust harder. She tightens her butt and all the muscles in her pelvis, feeling the pull that generates an orgasm. It's like anticipating an eruption and she's ready to welcome it. She bites him in his side and takes a hard grip of his cock while penetrating him even harder.

His whole body trembles before he explodes in a shuddering release, letting out a loud gasp. She can feel her own release and wetness dripping down her thigh.

They both collapse on the bed. A satisfied, tangled pile of pounding body parts, hot and sticky.